# Giants Don't Go Snowboarding

by Debbie Dadey
and
Marcia Thornton Jones

illustrated by John Steven Gurney

A
**LITTLE APPLE**
PAPERBACK

**SCHOLASTIC INC.**
New York   Toronto   London   Auckland   Sydney

*To Debbie Watts — MTJ*

*For Amanda Gibson, a great niece — DD*

No part of this publication may be reproduced in whole or in part, or stored in a retrieval system, or transmitted in any form or by any means, electronic, mechanical, photocopying, recording, or otherwise, without written permission of the publisher. For information regarding permission, write to Scholastic Inc., Attention: Permissions Department, 555 Broadway, New York, NY 10012.

ISBN 0-590-18983-2

24 23 22 21 20 19 18 17 16                                    3/0

Printed in the U.S.A.                                          40

First Scholastic printing, November 1998

# Contents

1. Vacation     1
2. Golden Egg     5
3. Milky White     10
4. Hugh Mongus     17
5. Fe-Fi     25
6. Giants     31
7. Doomed     35
8. War     42
9. Giant Problems     51
10. Golden Eggs     58
11. The Hen     63
12. The Last Mistake     68
13. Home for Christmas     73

# 1

# Vacation

"Geronimo!" Eddie screamed as he raced down the slope in Liza's backyard on his sled.

"Watch out for that tree!" Melody yelled to him. Eddie came dangerously close to a big maple tree before skidding to a stop. Thick snow covered every inch of Liza's backyard. The kids had been sliding down the hill for an hour and Eddie's face was almost as red as his hair.

"That was so cool," Eddie said. "I bet I hit fifty miles an hour."

"It wouldn't be cool if you knocked your head off," his friend Howie told him.

Melody giggled and pushed her black braids out of her face. "I bet your head

would roll down that hill at sixty miles per hour."

Eddie gave Melody a dirty look. "You're about as funny as Liza. Where is she anyway?"

Melody pointed to Liza's house. "Her mom called her inside to tell her something."

Just then Liza burst out the back door of her house. "Guess what?" she hollered.

"They canceled the rest of third grade," Eddie said, pulling his sled toward Liza.

Liza shook her head. "My mom is going on a ski vacation to the new lodge on Ruby Mountain. She's going to take skiing lessons."

"Big fat snowy deal," Eddie said. "Who cares?"

"You will," Liza said, "because she's taking all of us with her for a weekend vacation."

"Cool," Melody said.

"Skiing is expensive," Howie said. "I'm not sure my parents will let me go."

Liza held up her gloved hand. "The ski lodge is offering free snowboarding lessons this weekend. We can snowboard while Mom skis."

Eddie and Melody slapped Liza on the back. "Snowboarding is so neat," Eddie said. "I'll do flips all over the place."

"Flips?" Liza said. "That sounds dangerous."

Eddie put his gloves on his cheeks to get warm. "Snowboarding is as easy as throwing a snowball."

Howie put his hands on his hips. "Have you ever actually been snowboarding?" he asked Eddie.

"Well, no," Eddie admitted, "but it looks simple and it's free."

"I think I'll just watch," Liza said.

"You have to try it," Melody asked. "What's the worst that could happen?"

"I'm afraid to find out," Liza admitted.

# 2

# Golden Egg

"Joy to the world," Eddie sang from the back of Liza's van. The four kids and Liza's mom were riding to the ski lodge. Snow had started falling and the kids were singing Christmas songs since Christmas was only a few weeks away.

Instead of singing the rest of the song, Eddie burped it in perfect rhythm.

"That's disgusting," Liza told Eddie. "Christmas songs should be sung nicely."

"I'm only having a little fun," Eddie grumbled. "Don't get your mittens tied in a knot."

"Now that," Howie said, pointing out the car window, "looks like fun." The four kids peered out the window at the stone entrance to the Golden Egg Ski Lodge. Christmas lights twinkled in the trees around the entrance, but what amazed the kids was the snowboarder on a nearby slope.

"Wow!" Melody yelled. "He flipped upside down."

"He did it again," Howie said. "And he turned his whole body around twice."

"That's what I want to do," Eddie said. "I can't wait to get started."

The van rolled to a stop in front of the lodge and the snowboarder swished to a stop not far away. "Let's go meet him," Liza said. As the four kids tumbled out of the van, they heard a hollow clanging sound. It wasn't until they raced over to the short man that they realized a copper bell was dangling from the snowboarder's neck.

"That looks like a cowbell," Melody whispered to Liza.

"Shhh," Liza hissed. "He might hear you."

"Hello," Howie said to the man. "I'm Howie and these are my friends."

The man pushed back his goggles and smiled at the kids. "Hi," the man said. "My name is Jack. Are you here for the free snowboarding lessons?"

"You bet," Eddie said. "I want to do flips just like you."

Jack laughed. "I've been snowboarding a long time."

"I'm a fast learner," Eddie told him.

"Except in math," Melody said with a giggle.

Jack patted Eddie on the shoulder. "I'm the owner of the Golden Egg Ski Lodge, so if you need anything just ask me."

Jack helped the kids and Liza's mother with their bags. When the kids walked inside the lodge, they stopped to stare.

"This is really weird," Liza whispered.

# 3

## Milky White

The walls inside the lodge were decorated to look like a rustic barn. Every sofa and chair in the huge lobby was covered with black-and-white cow fabric. A small snack bar had black-and-white stools made to look like cows. There was even a life-sized stuffed cow next to a Christmas tree. The tree was decorated with twinkling lights and tiny white cow ornaments.

"I guess Jack likes cows," Melody said as Liza's mother checked into the lodge.

"It's pretty dumb-looking if you ask me," Eddie said, pretending to milk one of the stools.

Liza hopped onto a stool. "I think it is

MILKY WHITE

very cute," she said. "I hope our room is like this."

"I hope not," Eddie said. "I might throw up if I see another cow."

"But these are all the same cow," Melody pointed out. "Her name is even engraved on the frames."

"*Milky White*," Liza read from a nearby painting.

"That's a good name for a cow," Howie said.

Liza pointed to a painting in a gold frame. "This one is different," she said. The painting showed a giant chopping trees.

"We're not here to look at pictures," Eddie snapped. "Who cares about cows and giants anyway?"

"Eddie's right," Melody said. "Besides, here comes Jack. We can ask him about the pictures."

"Wait," Liza whispered. "I've heard of that cow, but I can't remember where."

But nobody was listening to Liza. They were reaching for the milk Jack carried on a tray.

"Help yourselves," Jack told them, holding out the tray.

"Do we have to pay for it?" Eddie blurted.

Melody jabbed her elbow into Eddie's ribs. "Don't be rude," she sputtered.

Jack didn't seem to mind. "You can have all the milk you want for free," he said. "There's nothing better than a cold glass of milk."

Eddie took his glass of milk before blurting out, "What's with all the giants and cows?"

Jack took a long drink of milk before answering. Then he shrugged. "Giants are fascinating," he finally said.

"Giants aren't even real," Eddie snapped. "How can they be interesting?"

"We can learn a lot from giants," Jack said seriously.

"How do you know so much about giants?" Howie asked.

"Studying giants helped me buy the Golden Egg Ski Lodge," Jack said before draining his glass. When he bent over to set his empty glass down, the bell around his neck clanged against the table.

"That's an interesting bell," Melody said. "I've never seen anybody wear a cowbell before."

Jack frowned and held the bell in his hand. "This bell," he said sadly, "belonged to my best friend. It helps me remember her."

"What happened to her?" Liza asked.

Jack sighed. "I lost her forever," he said. "I've looked and looked, but I'm afraid I'll never get her back."

"That's sad, but at least you have this lodge," Melody said.

Eddie wiped off his milk mustache. "Where did you come up with the name of Golden Egg Ski Lodge?"

Jack glanced around the lodge and

15

smiled. "I used my 'nest egg' to open this place. Golden Egg fits it perfectly."

Liza nodded. "I know all about 'nest eggs.' That's what my dad calls the account where he saves money for my college education."

Eddie rolled his eyes. "We'll never make it to college," he groaned. "We can't even make it through third grade!"

"Listen," Jack said. "You came here to learn snowboarding. And I have the perfect teacher!" Jack shook the cowbell hard. The floor started shaking and the chandelier over their heads swayed.

"Oh, no!" Howie yelled.

"It's an earthquake!" Eddie hollered.

The four kids were ready to run, but there was no place for them to go. Something was blocking the door. And it was huge!

# 4

## Hugh Mongus

Jack didn't bat an eyelash. He waved to the huge man standing in the doorway. The man was so big he had to duck to keep from hitting his head on the ceiling. In fact, everything about him was big, especially his ears. His bald head was shiny like a plastic Easter egg. Perched on top of his head was a pointy multicolored snowboarding hat.

"I'd like you to meet Hugh Mongus, the Golden Egg's snowboarding instructor," Jack said.

Hugh walked toward the kids. With every step he took, the floor shook and pictures on the wall rattled. He was almost in front of the kids when Hugh's feet got tangled in the rug. He tried to get his balance, but his hand hit the table.

Empty milk glasses crashed to the floor and Hugh landed in a big heap in front of the kids.

Jack sighed. "That's the tenth thing you've broken in less than a week," he said. "You are the clumsiest person I know."

Hugh struggled to sit up. When he sat on the floor he was almost the same height as Jack. "I'm sorry, boss," Hugh told Jack. "I tripped."

Hugh spoke with an English accent, and his voice was as deep as the snow on Ruby Mountain.

"You must be more careful," Jack said. Then he hurried off to find a broom.

Hugh smiled at the kids. "Are you ready to glide down Ruby Hill?" he asked.

"You mean Ruby Mountain," Howie said politely.

Hugh shook his head. "No," he said. "It's just a little hill to me. I'll show you." Hugh scrambled up from the floor and walked across the big lobby of the lodge. For every step he took, the kids had to take three. They were out of breath when Hugh finally stopped at a booth in the back corner of the lodge. A sign above the counter said SNOWBOARD SALES AND RENTALS. The kids almost didn't see it because of all the vines. In fact, the entire booth was covered with green tangled vines laced with twinkling lights. Hugh tripped over the vines to get to the other side of the counter.

"How may I help you?" Hugh asked as if he'd never seen the four kids in his entire life.

"Er . . ." Melody said, "we're here for snowboarding lessons."

Hugh slapped his forehead and giggled. "How silly of me. I forgot." Hugh pushed aside a clump of vines to uncover an ancient gold cash register. He punched buttons as if he were playing a Beethoven symphony on a piano. The cash register rang and clanged until the

drawer finally shot open and hit Hugh in the stomach.

"That will cost seven thousand, four hundred, ninety-eight dollars, and fifty-seven and a half cents," Hugh told them.

"Hey!" Eddie blurted. "This was supposed to be free."

"Besides," Howie said in his nicest voice, "there is no such thing as a half penny."

Hugh scratched his head and stared at the cash register for a full minute. Then he shrugged. "This machine always gets me confused," he admitted.

"You don't have to use a machine to figure out that free costs nothing," Eddie pointed out.

Hugh slapped his hand on the counter. When he did, the tangled mess of vines trembled. "You're right," Hugh said. "Now, why didn't I think of that? I'll get the snowboards."

WHACK! When Hugh reached for the

snowboards he bashed his head on the ceiling.

"Ouch," Melody whispered. "That had to hurt."

"Maybe he wears that goofy hat just to cover up all the bumps on his head," Eddie said with a snort.

"Don't be mean," Liza warned. "He can't help it if he's so tall and the ceiling gets in his way."

"No," Howie admitted. "But he can work on his clumsiness."

"Just because he tripped and bumped his head, it doesn't mean he's always clumsy," Melody said.

"His feet are just so big he can't help it," Liza said.

Hugh grabbed a snowboard. Unfortunately it got caught in the vines and Hugh tugged it free. When he did, it knocked into the rest of the snowboards and they all clattered to the floor like a row of dominoes.

"Okay," Melody admitted. "He's clumsy."

"And terrible at math," Eddie added.

"Be nice," Liza warned.

"I AM being nice," Eddie snapped. "After all, math is not my best school subject, but I had to help HIM figure out how much this was going to cost."

"That's only because you're an expert at free stuff," Howie told him.

"Shhh," Melody warned. "Here comes Hugh."

# 5

## Fe-Fi

"This is great!" Eddie shouted as they followed Hugh to the slopes. Hugh took such big steps, he was already far ahead of them. The kids had huge snowboards tucked under their arms and heavy boots on their feet. Eddie grinned even though it was hard to walk in the snow. "I'm finally going to fly through the air on a snowboard."

"I'd rather keep both my feet on the ground," Liza whined. "I wish I'd gone skiing with Mom."

"Where's your sense of adventure?" Melody asked Liza as snowflakes swirled around them.

Liza looked down at her clunky snow-boarding boots. "Adventure can be dan-

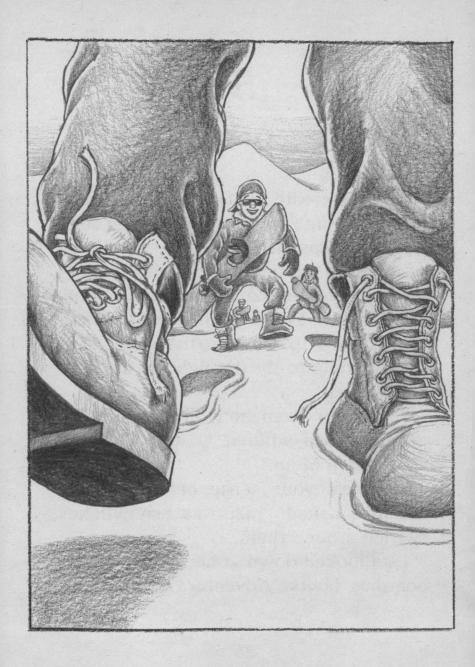

gerous. I think I'd rather read about it in a good book."

"Reading is good," Howie said, "but it doesn't take the place of a real live adventure."

Liza looked up at the big mountain slope ahead of them. "I just want to stay alive," she said with a lump in her throat.

"Shhh," Melody said. "I think Hugh said something to us." The four kids listened. They heard the wind blowing, but Hugh didn't say anything more.

"I think this cold weather is making you hear stuff," Eddie said, using one gloved hand to pull his hat farther down over his curly red hair.

"Shhh," Melody said. "There he goes again."

This time all the kids heard Hugh. He mumbled under his breath, "Fe-fi-fo-fum."

Eddie looked at Howie and laughed. Liza and Melody both giggled. "Did he say what I think he said?" Howie whispered, trying not to laugh. Eddie nodded and listened.

"Fe-fi-fo-fum," Hugh muttered again. Hugh talked to himself, paying no attention to the kids trailing behind.

"That reminds me of something I read in an old fairy tale," Liza said. "The one about a giant."

Eddie rolled his eyes. "I can't believe you still read silly stories like that."

Liza put one hand on a hip and stared at Eddie. "They aren't silly. You can learn things from fairy tales. Some are so sad they make me want to cry."

"All I have to do is look at you and it makes me want to cry," Eddie teased.

"Ha-ha." Liza pretended to laugh, then she stuck her tongue out at Eddie.

"You guys," Howie said, "this isn't funny. Hugh is gone."

"What are you talking about?" Melody said. "He was right in front of us."

Howie pointed ahead. "Well, he's not there now."

All the kids could see was snow, snow, and more snow. It fell around them in huge fluffy white flakes.

"I'm scared," Liza whimpered. "We'll be lost out here in the blizzard."

"This is not a blizzard," Eddie said. "We'll be fine." But just to be sure, Eddie stuck his snowboard into the ground and pulled it behind him.

"What are you doing?" Melody asked.

"I'm leaving a trail," Eddie said, "in case we can't find Hugh."

Howie nodded. "That's a great idea." He started dragging his snowboard behind him, also. Melody and Liza did the same. They walked in the direction that Hugh had been going. What the four friends didn't realize was that falling snow was quickly covering up their trail.

"What if we never find him?" Liza cried. "What if we freeze to death?"

"They can bury us with our snowboards," Eddie teased, "and use them for tombstones."

Liza looked ready to cry, but Melody put her hand on Liza's shoulder. "Don't worry," Melody said. "We'll be fine."

"Look," Howie said, pointing to the ground ahead. "I see something."

# 6

## Giants

"What is it?" Melody asked.

"Those are the biggest footprints I've ever seen," Liza said.

Eddie stuck his foot inside one of the large footprints. "Maybe these belong to Bigfoot," he said.

Howie shook his head. "No, these are bigger than the Bigfoot prints I saw in a library book." Howie put his foot inside the print with Eddie. So did Liza and Melody. The footprint held all four of the kids' feet.

"Whoever made these has huge feet," Melody said.

"Nobody can have feet that size," Liza said slowly, "unless they're a giant."

"Don't be silly," Melody said. "Giants are only in fairy tales."

"Or pro football," Howie said with a smile.

"I have a weird feeling about this," Liza said, pulling her friends away from the footprints. "I think there is something very strange going on around here."

Eddie nodded. "It's strange that you're in third grade and still believe in little fairies and giants."

Liza shook her finger at Eddie. "You don't know everything," she told him.

"Besides, why would a giant hide in Bailey City?" Howie asked.

Liza stared at the footprints, which were quickly being filled by the falling snow. "He's not hiding at all," she said. "He's right in front of our noses — or at least he was until he disappeared."

"Has your brain turned into icicles?" Eddie asked. "The only person around here was Hugh."

"Exactly," Liza said. "And Hugh is a giant."

Eddie burst out laughing. Howie and Melody couldn't help smiling.

Melody kicked her boot at the footprint. "Hugh isn't a giant, he just happens to be tall."

"Very, very tall," Howie added.

"He can't be a giant," Eddie told Liza. "After all, giants don't go snowboarding."

"How do you know that?" Liza asked. "Maybe giants like snowboards more than anything else in the whole world."

"I seriously doubt it," Melody said.

"But you don't know that for certain," Liza said.

Melody shrugged her shoulders. "No, I don't."

Howie looked up at the sky. "I know one thing," he said. "There is a terrible snowstorm brewing and we're right in the middle of it."

"Oh, my gosh," Liza squealed. "We'll be trapped on this mountain with a hungry giant. We're doomed!"

# 7

## Doomed

Eddie clutched his chest and staggered backward. "Liza's right," he gasped. "We ARE doomed. Doomed to stand here and listen to Liza yap about fairy tales."

Liza gave Eddie a shove and he ended up sitting in a pile of snow. "This is no joking matter," Liza warned.

"You're absolutely right," Eddie said, pounding the snow. "This is serious business."

"You mean," Melody said with wide eyes, "you believe Liza?"

"No," Eddie snapped as he jumped up and slapped snow from the seat of his pants. "I mean we're missing out on free snowboarding lessons all because of Liza."

"We can't go snowboarding now," Liza argued. "We're trapped in a blizzard on a mountain with a giant."

"The only blizzard on this mountain is happening inside your head," Eddie told her.

"But what about Hugh's big feet?" Liza said.

"Big feet don't mean anything," Melody pointed out. "After all, fashion models have some of the biggest feet I've ever seen."

"But it's just like in the fairy tale where a boy grew a magic beanstalk that reached all the way to the clouds," Liza told her friends. "There, he stole a giant's hen that laid golden eggs. When the giant tried to get his hen back, the beanstalk collapsed and he fell from his kingdom. He was trapped on earth."

Eddie put mitten-covered hands over his ears. "ARRRRGH!" he hollered. "Enough about giants and fairy tales and magic beans. I didn't come to Ruby

37

Mountain to listen to stories. I came here to snowboard!"

"Wait a minute," Melody said slowly. "Liza has a point."

"Don't tell me you believe her fairy-tale imagination!" Eddie begged.

Melody held up her hand. "I know the fairy tale Liza's talking about," she said. "The boy who stole the golden hen was named Jack."

"Exactly," Liza said. "The same as the owner of the Golden Egg Ski Lodge who said he built this ski lodge with his 'nest egg.'"

"And," Melody added, "the Jack in the story got his magic beans from selling a cow."

"AAHHHH!" Liza screamed.

"What's wrong?" Howie asked. "Are you in pain?" Howie planned to be a doctor when he grew up, so he was ready to help anybody in pain.

Liza pushed Howie away. "I just remembered something," she said.

Eddie nodded. "Sometimes using my brain hurts, too," he told Liza.

"I'm not in pain," Liza told him. "I'm scared. The cow in the story had a name."

"So?" Howie said. "My grandfather had cows on his farm, and he always gave them names."

"But the cow in the story," Liza said seriously, "was named Milky White."

"That's the name of the cow in all the pictures at the Golden Egg Ski Lodge," Howie said.

"Now you're getting it," Liza said.

"The only thing I'm getting is good and mad," Eddie said. "You can stand here and turn into snow statues if you want, but I'm going to march up that mountain and learn to snowboard."

Melody patted Liza's shoulder. "Eddie's right," she said. "Jack wouldn't send us up here if Hugh really was a kid-eating giant."

Just then a nearby tree rustled. Hugh pushed his way past the tree. "Fe-fi-fo-

fum!" he roared. "I thought I'd lost you. I had to backtrack to sniff you out. Follow me for the snowboarding adventure of your life!"

Eddie hurried to follow Hugh. Howie shrugged at Melody and headed after Eddie. Melody looked at Liza. "We'll be safe," Melody said, "as long as we stick together."

"I hope you're right," Liza said, "or we may end up as a giant's afternoon snack."

# 8

## War

A ski lift carried Hugh and the kids to the top of the slope. It had stopped snowing and the fresh blanket of snow made the mountain perfect for snowboarding. There, Hugh showed the kids how to balance on the snowboard. He taught them to twist back and forth. Then he let them try snowboarding on a short practice slope.

Howie went first. He hopped on his board and rode to the bottom of the slope like a pro. He only fell down once.

Melody was ready to go next, but Eddie pushed her aside. "Let me show you how," he bragged.

Eddie got on his board and immediately ended up sitting in the snow. His face was red, and it wasn't just from the cold. "No fair," he said. "I wasn't ready."

Eddie climbed on the snowboard again. This time, he stayed on — for at least two feet before the board slid out from under him and he ended up getting a mouthful of snow.

"I thought you said snowboarding was as easy as throwing a snowball," Melody said with a giggle as she passed Eddie, easily gliding down the beginners' hill on her snowboard.

"It is," Eddie yelled after her, "and if you keep yapping I'll prove it by aiming a snowball at you!"

Howie and Melody ignored Eddie as a towrope pulled them back to the top of the slope. They grinned at Eddie as they sailed by him to the bottom again. Eddie's face got redder and redder. Every time he tried to stand on his board, he lost his balance.

Liza patted Eddie's back. "This is

much harder than it looks," Liza told her friend. "I keep falling down, too."

Eddie kicked at a pile of snow. "This is a stupid sport," he sputtered. "These boards are better for surfing in the ocean than on snow."

Hugh grinned. "Here's something you can't do in the ocean." Hugh leaned over and scooped up a handful of snow. With his huge hands, he patted it into a perfect snowball. But Hugh's snowball was ten times bigger than a normal snowball.

"Let me see that," Eddie said. As soon as Hugh handed it to him, Eddie fell over in the snow. "Wow!" Eddie said. "It's heavier than it looks. Can you throw that thing?"

Hugh grinned. "Sure," he said. Then he sent his snowball sailing through the air. It landed with a thud in a pile of snow.

"This is great," Eddie said. "We'll make a winning team." Eddie bent over and scooped up his own snowball, took aim, and let it fly. It sailed through the air and landed right in the middle of Howie's back.

"WAR!" Howie yelled, and started scooping up snowballs. Melody and Howie stuck their snowboards in the snow and crouched low behind them. They scooped up snowballs and sent them in Eddie and Hugh's direction.

Hugh laughed so loud the tree limbs above his head shook. Then he joined

Eddie in lobbing snowballs at Melody and Howie.

Melody and Howie made snowballs as fast as they could, but just one of Hugh's snowballs was enough to make their snowboards fall over. Another snowball showered them with dusty snow. Eddie bombarded them while they were busy dodging Hugh's snowballs.

Liza stood in the shelter of a large spruce tree, watching the snowball fight.

"Help us, Liza!" Melody screeched. "We don't stand a chance against Hugh!"

"And that," Liza said to herself, "is exactly what I'm afraid of."

"We surrender!" Howie yelled. He was covered in snow from the top of his hat to the tip of his boots.

The kids waited for the lift back down to the lodge while Hugh gathered all the snowboards. "We were no match against Eddie's aim and Hugh's snowballs the size of Manhattan," Melody said.

Eddie grinned. "That was the snowball fight of my dreams," he said. "With Hugh on my side, I could conquer Bailey City."

Melody brushed snow from her pigtails and coat. "Why didn't you help us?" she asked Liza.

"You can't fight giants with snowballs," Liza told them simply.

"Are you still jabbering your giant junk?" Eddie sputtered. "You can't believe Hugh is really a giant."

"I'm more sure than ever," Liza told

him. "There are too many coincidences. The cow pictures, the beanstalk vines . . ."

"Your pea-sized brain," Eddie finished. "The only giant around here is you. You're a giant pain! Besides, I like Hugh. He's a lot of fun in a snowball fight."

"That's easy for you to say," Melody said. "You weren't trying to dodge his snow boulders."

"His snowballs were huge," Howie said slowly. "A normal person wouldn't be able to make them that big. Maybe we should listen to what Liza has to say."

Eddie grabbed Howie's shoulders and shook his friend. "Snap out of it," Eddie told Howie. "We're on Ruby Mountain in Bailey City, not in Liza's fairy-tale imagination."

Melody grabbed Eddie's arm. "There are too many things for us to ignore," she said. "If Hugh really is the giant, then that means he fell down the beanstalk and is trapped on Ruby Mountain."

Howie shrugged off Eddie's hands.

49

"We should think about what Liza said."

"I'll think about it," Eddie agreed, "as soon as Liza has proof."

"If proof is what you want," Liza said, "then proof is what you'll get."

"How do you plan to prove Hugh is a giant?" Melody asked.

"He's bound to give himself away," Liza said. "We just have to watch him long enough."

"Are you talking about spying?" Melody asked. "Because spying isn't a nice thing to do."

"That never stopped us before," Howie said.

"So you agree," Liza said. "We'll stake out Hugh. Then you'll see once and for all that the Golden Egg Ski Lodge comes complete with a giant."

# 9

# Giant Problems

The four kids hid in the shadows, behind couches, and under the tangled beanstalk vines once they got back to the lodge. They watched Hugh stack six pieces of bread together to make the biggest peanut butter sandwich the kids had ever seen. They saw Hugh turn on a tape player and listen to harp music. But they didn't see a single bit of giant evidence.

"This is stupid," Eddie whispered. "We should be out on the slopes."

"Shhh," Liza warned. "Here comes someone."

A couple stepped close to the counter. Hugh hurried to wait on them. When he did, he knocked over the table and his sandwich splattered on the floor.

The couple asked for skis and Hugh

punched his cash register buttons as if he were typing the words to a three-hundred-page book. When Hugh tried to charge the couple four thousand dollars, they nearly choked on their scarves until they finally figured out Hugh's mistake and paid with a hundred dollar bill.

Hugh reached in the cash register and gave the woman change for a thousand dollar bill. The woman looked at all the money in her hand, then gave it back and helped Hugh give her the right change.

"Wow," Eddie said. "Hugh is much better at making snowballs than at renting snowboards and skis."

"Giants," Howie said slowly, "are not known for being smart."

Liza nodded. "That's why they're so easy to trick."

"Whether he's a giant or not," Melody said, "he better watch out or he'll get in big trouble."

Melody was right. The kids weren't the

only ones watching Hugh. Jack was watching, too. As soon as the couple left with their skis, Jack stormed across the lobby. The cowbell around his neck clanged loudly when he slapped his hand on the counter right in front of Hugh. "I've had it!" Jack yelled. "Your mistakes are costing me money. If I see you make one more mistake, you're fired!" Then Jack marched away and disappeared through the swinging doors of the kitchen.

"It looks like Hugh has a giant problem of his own," Howie said. "We've got to help him."

"No, we don't," Eddie said. "You don't help me when I make mistakes during math, so we don't have to help Hugh. Besides, we came here to have fun."

"Hugh did teach us to snowboard," Liza said. "We should help him."

"Liza's right. It doesn't matter if someone's a giant or a princess," Melody said. "We should help anybody who needs it, and Hugh needs our help."

"Besides," Liza added, "if Hugh loses his job he won't have money to buy food. He might get hungry and start eating people. Then all of Bailey City would be in danger."

"Oh, brother," Eddie said, but nobody heard him because his friends had already scooted from their hiding places and were lined up at the snowboard counter.

Hugh sniffed again and looked at the kids. "May I help you?" he asked in a sad voice.

"No," Howie said, "but we can help you."

"You can?" Hugh asked.

Melody nodded. "We noticed you were having trouble with the cash register. We can show you how to make change."

"And we'll help you organize your counter," Liza said.

Hugh grinned and looked straight at Eddie. "You would do that for me?"

"Sure," Eddie said. "After all, you

helped us have fun on the slopes. Now we can help you."

Melody patted Eddie's back. "That's the spirit," she told him as they all started working.

It didn't take long for Liza and Eddie to straighten up the counter. Howie showed Hugh how to work the cash register. While Melody helped Hugh practice counting change, Howie helped Liza and Eddie untangle the mess of beanstalk vines curled around the counter.

"Wow," Eddie blurted out. "I bet these beanstalk vines would reach the sky if we can just get them untangled."

The change that Hugh was counting slipped through his fingers and clattered to the floor. He looked at Eddie for a full minute.

Then, a grin the size of a banana spread across Hugh's face, and he began to laugh.

# 10

## Golden Eggs

The kids were still untangling vines when they heard Jack's cowbell clanging across the lodge. Jack stopped at the front door and yelled back to Hugh. "I'm leaving to check on some valuables," Jack said. "Remember what I told you!" Then Jack left the lodge with a snowboard tucked under his arm.

"We have to get out of here," Liza squealed and threw on her coat.

"Now you're talking." Eddie smiled, waving good-bye to Hugh. "Let's go sledding."

Liza waited until her friends caught up with her. "No, we're not going sledding. We're following Jack. He said he was going to check on some valuables. I bet that's his stash of golden eggs."

"Cool," Melody said. "Maybe we can get one for Hugh in case he loses his job."

"Forget it," Eddie said. "If we get any golden eggs I'm keeping them. I could buy all sorts of cool stuff like video games."

"If we don't hurry Jack's going to get away," Howie said.

The four kids raced out the door. The snow fell like big fluffy feathers all around them. Mclody grabbed her snowboard from beside the entrance. "Let's take these in case we get to have some fun."

Eddie rolled his eyes. "Snowboarding is hard work," he complained, but he grabbed his snowboard anyway.

"There goes Jack," Howie said, pointing toward a tiny building behind the lodge. The four kids hurried after him with their snowboards, slipping and sliding on the hillside. Soon, the lodge was out of sight.

"This is crazy," Eddie fussed. "Why can't we just go sledding like normal kids?"

"Shhh," Melody hissed. "Jack is going into that little building."

"This is it," Liza said. "I bet this is where he keeps the hen that lays golden eggs. All we have to do is get a golden egg and give it to Hugh. Then his troubles will be over."

"Wouldn't that be stealing?" Howie asked.

Liza shook her head firmly. "No," she said. "The hen belonged to Hugh in the first place. So all the eggs are rightfully his."

Eddie laid his snowboard on the fresh snow, folded his arms, and looked at Liza. "Did you ever actually see any of these golden eggs?" he asked.

Liza's cheeks got beet red. "Well, not exactly."

"Then how do you know they're in that building?" Eddie asked.

"Well . . . I . . . um," Liza stuttered.

"In other words," Eddie said, "you don't know anything. We're out here in this snow freezing to death when we could be freezing to death and sledding."

*Boom!* Liza jumped and grabbed Eddie's arm. "What was that?" Liza squealed.

Melody patted Liza on the back. "Don't worry, it was only thunder," Melody said.

"This is really weird weather for December," Howie said. "First a snowstorm. Now thunder and here comes fog."

The kids stared at the ground. An eerie layer of white fog oozed around the trees and quickly enveloped their feet.

"I don't like this," Melody said with a shudder.

"Don't worry," Liza told her friends. "Remember what Jack told us about giants? This is perfectly normal weather . . . when you're in giant country."

"Shhh," Melody said. "I hear something and it's definitely not thunder."

# 11

## The Hen

"Hide!" Liza whispered before scrambling around the side of the building. Her three friends watched Jack leave the cabin and head back down the hillside. His jacket pockets bulged.

"Look," Liza whispered. "He has the golden eggs."

"I want those eggs," Eddie said. "I could do some serious toy shopping with one of those babies."

"Will you stop arguing?" Mclody said. "If there really is a hen that lays golden eggs inside this building then there's only one thing to do."

"What?" Eddie asked.

Melody checked to make sure Jack had disappeared down the slope before

heading to the building's door. "It's easy," she said. "We'll just go inside and get some." Melody pulled on the door, but it was locked.

"Smooth move," Eddie teased. "Have any other brilliant ideas?"

Liza looked at the ground near the door. There appeared to be a small hole. "Maybe we can dig our way in," she suggested. Liza and Eddie dropped to their knees and pawed the snow away with their mittens.

"It's hopeless," Liza said, sitting back on her heels.

"Besides, the ground under the snow is frozen solid," Eddie complained.

"If we can't go under," Liza said slowly, "maybe we can go over."

"What are you talking about?" Melody asked.

Liza pointed to a high window in the tiny building. "I bet one of us could fit through that window."

"Yeah," Eddie sneered. "If one of us

was six feet tall. There's no way we can reach that."

"You could if you stood on Howie's back," Melody said.

Eddie shook his head. "No way."

Melody folded her arms over her chest. "I thought you wanted to buy lots of toys."

"Of course I do," Eddie admitted.

Liza smiled. "If you do this I'm sure Hugh will reward you."

Eddie groaned. "All right, I'll do it." Howie bent down under the window and Eddie scrambled onto his back. With Liza's and Melody's help, Eddie stood up on Howie's back.

Eddie's hands were on the window frame when thunder boomed again. Howie jumped and Eddie lost his footing. Eddie fell right onto Melody.

"Ahhhh!" Melody screamed and started sliding backward down the hillside. Eddie slid right after her.

"Oh, my gosh," Liza squealed. "They're heading right for Jack!"

# 12

## The Last Mistake

Melody tried to stop, but the snow was too slick. She slid into Jack's legs, knocking his snowboard from his hands. It twirled three times in the air before landing back in the snow — right in Eddie's path.

"Look out!" Liza screamed. But there was nothing Eddie could do. He tumbled down the slope and landed belly-first on Jack's snowboard. Before anyone could say "fe-fi-fo-fum" Eddie was soaring down the slope like a professional snowboarder, only on his tummy.

"He's heading straight for the lodge!" Liza screamed. "What should we do?"

"There's only one thing we can do," Howie said. "We have to stop him."

Howie hopped on his own snowboard

and sped down the hill after Eddie. Liza gulped. Then she jumped on her snowboard and pushed off through the snow.

As soon as Melody and Jack saw what was happening, they hurried to get Melody's and Eddie's snowboards and then they raced down the hill, too.

They were all going as fast as they could, but they weren't fast enough. Eddie sped down the hill as if he were an Olympic gold-medal racer. He zipped past Liza's mother, who was taking her ski lesson.

"Look out below!" Eddie yelled as he dodged three skiers and hurtled past the ski lodge. Everybody at the Golden Egg Ski Lodge stopped to stare.

Hugh ran across the snow. Liza's mother skied over to Eddie as fast as she could. Howie and Liza snowboarded after Eddie. Melody and Jack came next. But when they reached Eddie, all they saw were two boots sticking up out of the snow.

Hugh bent down, grabbed Eddie's boots, and pulled. Eddie popped out of the snowbank like a cork.

"Are you all right?" Liza's mother gasped.

Eddie grinned. "That was more fun than riding a roller coaster."

"I'm sorry," Melody apologized to Jack. "We didn't mean to knock you down."

Jack patted his pockets. They still bulged. "No harm done," Jack told them. "Everything is fine. I believe all this excitement calls for a big glass of milk."

Hugh grinned. "That sounds delicious! I'll lead the way."

As they all filed after Hugh and Jack, Liza tugged on Melody's sleeve. "Did you hear that?" Liza said. "The eggs in Jack's pocket didn't break. They must be golden."

"Just because they didn't break doesn't mean they're made from gold," Howie whispered.

"Maybe they're frozen solid," Eddie said.

Liza was ready to argue, but just then, Hugh forgot to duck and he bumped his head on the lodge door. When he did, he fell backward, right on top of Jack. They both landed in a big pile on the ground.

Jack's hands flew to his pockets and his face turned white like the snow. "That," Jack told Hugh, "was your last mistake!"

# 13

## Home for Christmas

The next morning, Liza woke up early. She was worried about Hugh. "What is going to happen to Hugh?" she asked her friends as they hurried to the lobby. "Jack was really angry yesterday."

Eddie nodded. "He even forgot to give us our free milk."

"Stop thinking about free milk," Howie said to Eddie. "Worry about Bailey City."

Melody nodded. "If there's one thing Bailey City doesn't need, it's a hungry giant on the loose. We'd better hope nothing happened to Hugh."

"I do hope nothing happened to him," Eddie told his friends, "because I want him to help me make a huge snow fort so I can whip you in a snowball war."

The kids rushed to the lobby, but Hugh

was nowhere to be found. "Oh, no," Melody cried. "Jack got rid of him."

"No, he didn't," Liza said. She smiled and pointed to a window. The beanstalk vines that once curled around Hugh's snowboard counter were no longer a tangled mess. Now, they stretched across the lobby and out a nearby window.

The four kids hurried outside. The beanstalk wound around the chimney, draped into the branches of a spruce tree, and disappeared into the clouds.

"Hugh found his way home," Liza said, "so I guess I'll never be able to prove he was really a giant."

"I'll prove it," Eddie said, putting a foot on the beanstalk. "All we have to do is follow him up this beanstalk."

"Oh, no you don't," Jack said as he carried an ax over to the beanstalk. "This is what I do best," Jack said. The kids stood back as Jack lifted the ax high above his head. With three heavy swings, Jack

chopped down the beanstalk. Then Jack turned and marched into the Golden Egg Ski Lodge.

Liza sighed. "I guess we'll never know for sure that Hugh was a giant," she said.

"It won't be the same without Hugh around," Eddie said seriously, "but we should be happy for Hugh because he got to go home for Christmas."

The rest of the kids stared at Eddie before Howie broke the silence. "I thought the only thing you cared about was playing in the snow."

"Besides," Melody added, "you said you didn't believe in giants."

Eddie shrugged. "I'll only admit one thing: Giants don't go snowboarding and only crazy people ride boards."

Then Eddie reached down, grabbed a pile of snow, and bombarded his friends with his own giant snowballs.